MW01180587

104

WITHDRAWN

*Many Cultures,
One World*

Ireland

by Kay Melchisedech Olson

Consultant:
Patrick O'Donnell
Composition and Literature Instructor
Normandale Community College
Bloomington, Minnesota
and
Contributing Writer
Irish Gazette
St. Paul, Minnesota

Blue Earth Books

an imprint of Capstone Press
Mankato, Minnesota

Blue Earth Books are published by Capstone Press
151 Good Counsel Drive, P.O. Box 669, Mankato, Minnesota 56002
http://www.capstone-press.com

Library of Congress Cataloging-in-Publication Data
Olson, Kay Melchisedech.
  Ireland / by Kay Melchisedech Olson.
    p. cm.—(Many cultures, one world)
  Summary: An introduction to the geography, culture, and people of Ireland. Includes a map, legend, recipe, craft, and game.
  Includes bibliographical references and index.
  ISBN 0–7368–2168–6 (hardcover)
  1. Ireland—Juvenile literature. [1. Ireland.] I. Title. II. Series.
DA906.O45 2004
941.5—dc21   2003000061

Editorial credits

Editor: Katy Kudela
Series Designer: Kia Adams
Photo Researcher: Alta Schaffer
Product Planning Editor: Karen Risch

Cover photo of Irish countryside, by Stockbyte

Capstone Press thanks Nikki L. Ragsdale, designer, writer, editor,
and member of the Northern California Irish Network, for help in
preparing the text of this book.

Photo credits

Bruce Coleman Inc./Hand Reinhard, 23
Capstone Press, 21 (bottom); Gary Sundermeyer, 3 (middle, bottom),
    17 (right), 19, 29
Corbis/Adam Woolfitt, 13 (right); Paul A . Souders, 16–17, 24–25;
    Dave Bartruff, 21 (left); Yann Arthus-Bertrand, 25 (right);
    Tim Thompson, 27 (right)
Eileen R. Herrling, 26–27
Getty Images/Hulton Archive, 11
One Mile Up Inc., 21 (top)
PhotoDisc Inc./Siede Preis, 10
Richard Cummins, 4–5, 8, 9, 14–15, 15 (right), 22
Richard Cummins/The Viesti Collection Inc., 12–13
Stockbyte, 6, 18, 20
Visuals Unlimited/Brian Rogers, 28

1 2 3 4 5 6 08 07 06 05 04 03

Contents

Turn to page 7 to find a map of Ireland.

Check out page 23 to learn how to play an Irish game.

See page 19 to learn how to make a favorite Irish treat.

Look on page 29 to find out how to grow a leprechaun.

CHAPTER 1

Welcome to Ireland

The color green covers Ireland like a patchwork quilt. Stone fences look like stitches holding patches of green cloth together. Ireland's landscape is so green that it is known as the "Emerald Isle."

Ireland is an island slightly larger than the U.S. state of West Virginia. It is located west of Great Britain, which once ruled all of Ireland. In 1922, Ireland was divided into two sections. Northern Ireland became part of the United Kingdom, along with England, Scotland, and Wales.

Stone fences stretch across Ireland's green countryside.

Facts about Ireland

Name: ....Republic of Ireland

Capital: ....Dublin

Population: ....3,917,336 people

Size: ....27,135 square miles
.......................(70,280 square kilometers)

Languages: ....English, Gaelic (Irish)

Religion: ....Roman Catholic Church
.......................of Ireland

Highest point: ...Carrantuohill, 3,414 feet
.......................(1,041 meters)

Lowest point: ...Atlantic Ocean, sea level

Main crops: ....Barley, sugar beets, wheat,
.......................potatoes, turnips

Money: ....Euro

The Republic of Ireland is an independent country. It has a democratic form of government. Dublin is its capital. About 4 million people live in the Republic of Ireland.

Ireland's countryside combines many landscapes. There are rolling hills, green meadows, and steep rocky cliffs. The Shannon River runs 240 miles (386 kilometers) through the middle of Ireland. It is the longest river in Ireland. Large areas of Ireland are covered by peat bogs. These areas are wet and soggy. People cut the wet peat and stack it in blocks to dry. During winter, they burn peat for heating fuel.

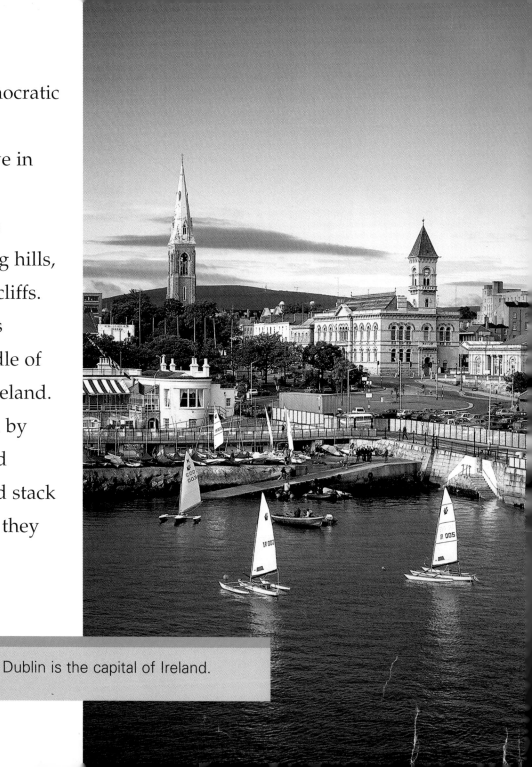

Dublin is the capital of Ireland.

Map of Ireland

ATLANTIC
OCEAN

SCOTLAND

ENGLAND

NORTHERN
IRELAND

IRELAND

Shannon River

Irish Sea

Dublin ⭐

Cliffs of
Moher

WALES

Carrantuohill

Waterford ●

Cork ●

Legend

⭐ Capital City
● City
◆ Cliffs of Moher
🜋 Highest Point
〜 River

N
W E
S

CHAPTER 2

Irish Legends

Saint Patrick is the patron saint of Ireland. Each year on March 17, Irish people around the world celebrate Saint Patrick's Day. Patrick was a Roman Catholic priest and later a bishop. More than 1,000 years ago, he preached the Christian faith to people throughout Ireland. Around the year A.D. 461, Patrick died. Later, the Catholic Church made Patrick a saint.

Many people believe Patrick died on March 17. In his honor, people celebrate Saint Patrick's Day. People

Saint Patrick is important to the people of Ireland. He is shown in many types of art, such as stained glass.

celebrate this holiday with parades, food, and music.

Patrick was a real person. He was born in Scotland in the late A.D. 300s. As a young boy, Patrick was kidnapped and sold as a slave in Ireland. He learned the Irish language before escaping. Patrick went to live in Britain.

Patrick had a very strong belief in God. He joined the Catholic Church as a deacon, helping the priests. When Patrick became a priest himself, Pope Celestine sent him back to Ireland. The pope wanted Patrick to bring the teachings of Jesus Christ to the Irish people.

Many legends tell of Saint Patrick's deeds in Ireland. Legends are stories that have some truth in them. But usually legends make a true story seem more important than it really is.

Legend of the Leprechaun

Irish legend says that leprechauns are little men with magical powers. Leprechauns guard pots of gold. Should a person ever catch a leprechaun, the leprechaun will trade his gold for freedom. Leprechauns believe that humans are silly, greedy creatures.

Some signs in Ireland remind people of the famous leprechaun legend.

After becoming a priest, Patrick went back to Ireland to teach the Christian faith. Christians believe God is three divine people in one. It was hard for people to understand this idea called the Holy Trinity. They did not see how God could be Father, Son, and Holy Spirit all in one.

Believing in miracles, Saint Patrick prayed. He bowed his head and closed his eyes. He asked God to help him make the people understand. When he finished praying, Saint Patrick opened his eyes. The first thing he saw was a three-leaf clover growing at his feet.

He picked the shamrock clover and held it up for all to see. "I am holding this shamrock by its one stem," Saint Patrick said. "But you can see there are three leaves to this one shamrock. So God is with the Holy Trinity."

The shamrock is a symbol of Ireland.

The legend of Saint Patrick and the snakes is the most famous Irish legend. Long ago, thousands of snakes crawled all over the Emerald Isle. People turned to Saint Patrick to rid their homes of the pesky snakes.

No one knows exactly how Saint Patrick tricked the snakes. Some people say he went to a mountain and rang a bell. Others say he stood by the ocean and began beating a drum. However he did it, Saint Patrick made enough noise to annoy the snakes. They soon crawled into the sea, where every snake drowned. People still tell this legend to explain why there are no wild snakes anywhere in Ireland.

According to legend, Saint Patrick rid Ireland of all its snakes.

CHAPTER 3

City and Country Life

More people live in Irish cities and towns than in the countryside. Colorful row houses are common in Irish cities. These homes are built one after the other in a row. They have no space in between. Many other people live in apartments.

Cottages are common homes in the Irish countryside. Most Irish people who live in the countryside are farmers. The farms are small. Ireland's green meadows are good for livestock. Many farmers raise cows, horses, and sheep.

Brightly colored row houses line the streets of Ireland's cities.

Potatoes in Ireland

Potatoes have always been an important crop in Ireland. Between 1845 and 1848, a fungus destroyed almost all of the potatoes in Ireland. More than 1 million people died from starvation during this potato blight. Thousands of Irish people left the country. Many moved to the United States, Canada, England, and Australia.

Many farmers in Ireland grow potatoes.

CHAPTER 4

Seasons in Ireland

Ireland's four seasons are similar in temperature. July has the highest average temperature of 61 degrees Fahrenheit (16 degrees Celsius). The lowest average temperature of 36 degrees Fahrenheit (2 degrees Celsius) comes in January.

Ireland has 175 to 200 days of rain a year. April and May are the driest months in Ireland. More than half of Ireland's rain falls between August and January. The greatest rainfall is in the southwest.

Ireland's many rain showers create small waterfalls in streams.

Ireland's Rainy Days

Ireland has one of the wettest climates in western Europe. Much of Ireland's rain falls as a fine mist. Irish people call this type of misty day with rain a "soft day." A colorful rainbow might appear in the sky on a rainy day in Ireland.

CHAPTER 5

Family Life in Ireland

Typical Irish families include a father, mother, and three to four children. The father is the wage earner in most Irish families. Irish mothers usually are homemakers. Some Irish women work outside the home. Children are expected to study hard in school. They help their parents at home.

Most families in Ireland are Roman Catholic. Families attend church together on Sundays and special holy days.

Most families in Ireland have three to four children.

Birthdays in Ireland

Irish children have a special birthday custom. Friends give the birthday child "bumps." They hold the birthday child upside down. They gently bump the person's head on the floor the number of times to match the birthday child's age. They add one last bump for luck.

Christmas, Easter, and Saint Patrick's Day are the most important religious holidays in Ireland.

Irish food is simple but filling. Potatoes, cabbage, and dairy products are served at most meals. Boxty is a common potato dish. Boxty is a shredded potato pancake fried in butter. Irish people also eat corned beef and cabbage at many meals.

Families enjoy music, sports, and other activities together. The neighborhood pub is a gathering place for Irish people. They come to the pubs to talk, eat, drink, and listen to music.

Irish football is a favorite sport in Ireland. It is played like soccer, but players may touch the ball with their hands. Hurling is another popular Irish sport. Players use sticks to hit a ball into a goal.

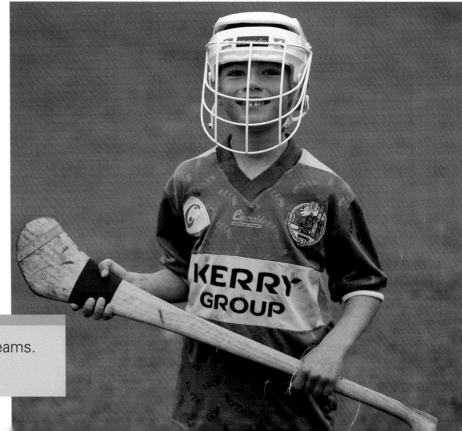

Children in Ireland play on hurling teams. Hurling is a favorite sport in Ireland.

Irish Tea Bread

Tea time is an important part of the day in Ireland. Morning tea is served about 11:00 in the morning. Afternoon tea is served between 3:00 and 5:00 in the afternoon. High tea is really the evening meal. It is served about 6:00 or later at night.

You can make this Irish tea bread for afternoon tea or as a dessert for high tea. Serve the bread with tea, milk, or hot chocolate.

What You Need

Ingredients
¾ cup (175 mL) strong tea
1 pound (455 grams) diced dried fruit
¾ cup (175 mL) soft brown sugar
1 egg (lightly beaten)
2 tablespoons (30 mL) melted butter
1¼ cups (300 mL) flour
½ teaspoon (2.5 mL) baking soda

Equipment
bowl with cover
dry-ingredient measuring cups
large mixing spoon
large loaf pan
baking parchment paper
nonstick cooking spray
mixing bowl
measuring spoons
pot holders
wire cooling rack

What You Do

1. Mix tea, dried fruit, and sugar in a bowl. Cover and let sit overnight.
2. Line the bottom of a large loaf pan with baking parchment paper. Apply nonstick cooking spray to inside of pan. Set aside.
3. Preheat the oven to 350°F (180°C).
4. In a bowl, stir together the egg and melted butter with mixing spoon.
5. Stir flour and baking soda into the egg mixture.
6. Add the tea, dried fruit, and sugar to the mixture. Stir batter well.
7. Pour the batter into the pan. Smooth the top.
8. Bake on the middle rack of the oven for 1 to 1½ hours or until dark brown.
9. Use pot holders to remove the pan from the oven and let pan cool 2 to 3 minutes.
10. Gently turn the bread loaf out of the pan onto a wire cooling rack. Cool before serving.

Makes 10 slices

CHAPTER 6

Laws, Rules, and Customs

Irish law orders all children ages 6 to 15 to attend school. From ages 6 to 12, children attend first-level schools. Students go to second-level schools until about age 17. Many young people attend a university or technical college after finishing a second-level school.

Most elementary school children in Ireland attend schools run by the Catholic Church. Children study math, reading, writing, and other subjects. They also learn about their religion.

The Law in Ireland

- Irish police officers do not carry guns.
- It is against the law to kill swans in Ireland.
- Until 1995, no one was allowed to get a divorce in Ireland.
- Murphy is a common last name in Ireland. Murphy's Law is really just a saying. It means, "If anything can go wrong, it will."

The swan is protected by Irish laws.

Many Irish schoolchildren attend Catholic schools.

Ireland's national flag has three stripes of green, white, and orange. The green and the orange stand for two sides fighting against each other. The white in the middle stands for peace between the two sides.

Ireland and England are the two sides who have fought against each other. The green stripe on the flag stands for old Ireland, which is known as the Emerald Isle. Orange stands for Protestants in honor of the English King called William of Orange. Ireland's flag was first used in 1848.

Today, Ireland's money is the euro. Ireland and 10 other countries in Europe began using this money in 1999. Euros come in paper notes and coins. One hundred cents equals a euro.

Before using the euro, Ireland's money was the Irish pound. It was also called the punt.

Classes are taught in the English language. But Irish students must learn Gaelic. It is the oldest language in Ireland. Children also learn about Ireland's culture. They read traditional stories and sing Irish folk songs.

Some children know the art of traditional Irish dance.

Play the Dead Fox Game

This game is a favorite of many Irish children. In this game, the word "wake" does not mean to wake up. In Ireland, family and friends gather at a wake when someone has died. They stay up all night with the body of their loved one. At a wake, people often pass the time singing and telling stories. In the game, the children are "waking" the fox.

You can play this game with friends or classmates. Follow the "How to Say It" guide, and learn to speak Gaelic while having fun.

What You Need
six or more children
plenty of room (indoors or out)

What You Do
1. Stand in a circle with one person in the center.
2. The center person lies down, pretending to be a dead fox.
3. The rest of the players walk around the "fox," going as near as they dare chanting the words listed in the "How to Say It" guide.
4. During the chant, the "dead fox" suddenly springs up and chases the other players in the circle.
5. Whoever is caught becomes the next "dead fox."

Irish Gaelic	How to Say It	English
Madra rua marbh,	MAHD-ra ROO-uh MAH-roo	Dead fox,
is deacair é a thórramh;	iss JACK-ur ay uh HO-roo	he's hard to wake;
i'íosfadh sé cearca	JEE-soo shay KYARK-uh	he'd eat the hens and
'gus lachain na gcomharsan.	guss LAKH-un nuh GOOAR-san	ducks of the neighbors.

CHAPTER 7

Pets in Ireland

Cats and dogs are the most popular pets in Ireland. About twice as many people have cats as pets than dogs. But dogs have been kept as pets in Ireland longer than any other animal.

Other interesting pets are kept in Ireland. A few Irish pet stores offer snakes for sale. Some people choose baby corn snakes, jungle pythons, milk snakes, and other reptiles for pets. Parrots are also kept as pets in some Irish homes.

Cats are a favorite pet in Ireland.

Irish Pet Names

Some names have always been popular for Irish dogs. Many people also use these same names for other dogs, cats, birds, snakes, horses, and hamsters.

Irish Pet Name	How to Say It	What It Means
Dubh	DUV	Black
Bainín	BAWN-een	White
Madra	MOD-ra	Dog
Cú	COO	Hound
CúChulainn	koo-CHUL-in	A legendary Irish hero
Dearg	DARR-ig	Red
Rua	ROO-a	Red

The Irish wolfhound is a popular breed of dog in Ireland.

CHAPTER 8

Sites to See in Ireland

Tourism is an important industry in Ireland. The country's tourism trade slogan is "Cead Mile Fáilte." It means "A hundred thousand welcomes." Ireland welcomes about 7 million visitors each year.

Some people come to Ireland to see the ruins of old buildings and castles. Blarney Castle is located near Cork, Ireland's second largest city. The Blarney Stone can be found near the top of the castle. Visitors who kiss the Blarney Stone are said to be

The Blarney Castle and other castles are common in Ireland's countryside.

Visitors who kiss the Blarney Stone lie flat on their backs. They hold onto iron railings and kiss the stone upside down.

able to talk easily without worry or embarrassment.

Steep cliffs and stone monuments are also popular with tourists. Some people come to see the Cliffs of Moher. These cliffs stretch 5 miles (8 kilometers) on the edge of the Atlantic Ocean. They drop about 650 feet (198 meters) straight down to the ocean.

Irish cities also attract many tourists. Dublin is Ireland's largest city. Trinity College, a university founded in 1592, is located there. It contains the Book of Kells, one of the oldest books in the world. Waterford is Ireland's third largest city. Waterford crystal is made in a factory here. This glassware is famous around the world.

The Cliffs of Moher drop steeply to the Atlantic Ocean.

Grow a Leprechaun

The leprechaun legend is popular in Ireland. Leprechauns are said to be little men who work as shoemakers. They wear green hats with black bands and gold buckles. Their name may have come from the Gaelic word for shoemaker, "leath bhrogan."

You can make a funny little leprechaun. Pretend that the paper hat he wears is magic. Make believe the grass is green hair growing out of the top of his hat.

What You Need

small plastic foam cup
large wiggle eyes (two)
glue
red marking pen
construction paper (black, green, and yellow)
scissors
potting soil (or garden dirt)
1 to 2 teaspoons (5 to 10 mL) grass seed
measuring spoon
water

What You Do

1. Glue wiggle eyes side by side on the lower half of the plastic cup.
2. With marking pen, draw mouth in place under the eyes.
3. Make a leprechaun hat from the construction paper. Test the hat to make sure it fits at the top of the cup. Set it aside.
4. Carefully fill the cup with potting soil to about ½ inch (1.2 centimeters) from the top.
5. Sprinkle grass seed over the top of the potting soil.
6. Use your finger to gently mix the grass seed into the soil.
7. Brush off any soil that may have spilled on the outside of the cup.
8. Put the leprechaun hat in place at the top of the cup. If the hat covers the area where the grass will grow, cut a little off the top of the hat.
9. Carefully water the grass seed with 1 to 2 teaspoons (5 to 10 mL) of water every day.
10. Watch as the leprechaun's "hair" seems to magically grow out of the hat.
11. Use scissors to give the leprechaun a haircut if the grass grows too long.

Words to Know

blight (BLITE)—a disease that destroys plants

bog (BOG)—an area of wet, spongy land

divine (duh-VINE)—to do with or from God, or a god

emerald (EM-ur-uhld)—a bright green precious stone

fungus (FUHN-guhss)—a type of plant that has no leaves, flowers, or roots

Gaelic (GAY-lik)—the language of Ireland

patron saint (PAY-truhn SAYNT)—a person honored by the Christian Church for leading a holy life; some people believe a patron saint looks after a country or group of people; Saint Patrick is the patron saint of Ireland.

peat (PEET)—dark brown, partly decayed plant matter that is found in bogs and swamps

shamrock (SHAM-rok)—a small, green plant with three leaves

To Learn More

Banting, Erinn. *Ireland the Culture.* The Lands, Peoples, and Cultures Series. New York: Crabtree, 2002.

Cummins, Richard. *Ireland.* Let's Investigate. Nations. Mankato, Minn.: Creative Education, 2001.

Deady, Kathleen W. *Ireland.* Countries of the World. Mankato, Minn.: Bridgestone Books, 2001.

Ryan, Patrick. *Ireland.* Faces and Places. Chanhassen, Minn.: Child's World, 2000.

Useful Addresses

Embassy of Ireland
2234 Massachusetts Avenue NW
Washington, DC 20008

Erin Go Bragh Foundation
37 Clinton Road
Glen Ridge, NJ 07028

Irish American Heritage Center
4626 North Knox Avenue
Chicago, IL 60630

Irish American Heritage Museum
2267 Route 145
East Durham, NY 12423

Internet Sites

Do you want to find out more about Ireland?
Let FactHound, our fact-finding hound dog, do the research for you.

Here's how:

1) Visit ***http://www.facthound.com***
2) Type in the **Book ID** number: **0736821686**
3) Click on **FETCH IT.**

**FactHound will fetch Internet sites picked
by our editors just for you!**

Index